a novella

hopeless
the woman with
the issue of blood

a novella

hopeless

the woman with the issue of blood

GOLDEN KEYES PARSONS

WhiteFire
Publishing

HOPELESS: THE WOMAN WITH THE ISSUE OF BLOOD

WhiteFire Publishing
13607 Bedford Rd NE
Cumberland, MD 21502

ISBN: 978-1-939023-20-9 (print)
       978-1-939023-21-6 (digital)

To women who might have felt trapped, or alone,
or who needed forgiveness or healing—
who felt as if no one cared, or even knew their names.
An encounter with Jesus turned women's lives around
then—
and meeting Him still does today.

Dear Reader,

This series about nameless women in Scripture has been in my heart for 30 years. I wrote the first book about the adulterous woman approximately that long ago. I was an amateur writer then and made many mistakes on the technical side of the craft, but the story was there. And I kept pitching the idea to publishers and editors, but at that time the popularity of biblical fiction was waning. Or more well-known authors had a series out there that was too similar. But the series wouldn't let me go. It seemed interesting to me that some of the major encounters Jesus had in his ministry were with women, and that those women were not even named in the accounts. However, they were important enough to be included in the canon.

In the meantime, I got a contract for another series, based on my family genealogy in 17th century France, the Darkness to Light series, and subsequently published a Civil War novel set in Texas, *His Steadfast Love*. One day via a writers loop I learned that WhiteFire Publishing was interested in biblical fiction. They bought the series and they are now reality.

I hope you will find touchstones in these stories that will ring true to you as a woman. Jesus broke many cultural and social mores of the day to relate to women—women who felt trapped by laws and tradition; those who needed forgiveness; some who had been abused.

I love to hear from my readers. You may contact me through my web site at www.goldenkeyesparsons.com or by email at golden@goldenkeyesparsons.com.

May the One who has our names engraved on the palm of His hand minister to you through these novellas.

Blessings,
Golden Keyes Parsons

Red. Thick and slimy. Surrounding her. Smothering her. Choking her. Zahava swam her way to consciousness through the red, oozing stream. She sat up and realized she had been moaning in her sleep. The fever made her tremble, and she reached for the blanket bunched at her feet, pulled it to her chin, and continued to shiver underneath the scratchy threads. Her teeth chattered.

Gideon turned over and continued his soft snoring.

Ever since Zahava could remember, fever produced the same dream. It started with a line drawn horizontally across her mind with people walking along it, step by plodding step, their shoulders slumped forward. She watched them as they moved across her mind's eye from right to left in a clump. Their legs moved, but they never left her sight—always moving, trying to reach something, somewhere in the distance, but never making any progress. A red trickle of blood oozed from the ground and pooled around her. It moved like a living thing toward the people, gaining momentum as it seeped toward them. The whirling, swirling eddy engulfed Zahava's feet and thrust her toward the people. It swallowed all of them in its sticky grip. If she could just reach that mysterious object in the distance, she knew she could escape the blood. But she never could. She always jolted awake as the suffocating liquid engulfed her.

She lay back on her pillow and covered her face with her arm. Sweat beaded on her lip. She wiped her face with the sleeve of her tunic and ran her hand over her swollen belly. Was their baby well? She prayed this current malady wouldn't affect the soon-to-arrive infant. This was their firstborn. She didn't know how she was supposed to feel, couldn't tell if anything was awry. Her mother and mother-in-law both reassured her everything was fine.

A smile tugged at her lips as she felt the baby move within her. Only a few more weeks, and they would know whether she carried a son or a daughter. She prayed it was a boy. A firstborn son made for a proud father, set the inheritance in good order. Then they could have a daughter later on for her.

As the oldest daughter, Zahava had taken care of little ones all of her growing-up years. Her mother had birthed ten children—a healthy, robust brood from the moment they were born, and they came rapid fire, one after another. By the time her mother got the last one up and walking, along came another little mouth to feed. And Zahava carried the littlest brother or sister on her hip as her mother nursed the newest baby.

She tried to feel her hip bone through her expanding waistline. Still there. Soon she would be hoisting her own little one onto her hip.

She rolled over and watched her husband sleep. Gideon looked more boy than man when he slept. His dark hair curled around his face, thick and shiny. She loved when he wore his hair long, but since they married he'd kept it cut shorter. He was young. Neither of them were twenty yet. But she was certain he would be a good father to their new baby. She brushed his hair away from his face with the tips of her fingers.

The eastern sky displayed soft pink through the archways

from the balcony of their quarters in the rear of his parents' considerable estate. They would add on rooms as their family grew. As soon as the sun rose every morning, so did her husband, with a smile on his face, eager to get to work in his family's import/export business. Her father had made a good match for her.

Gideon's eyes fluttered open. He smiled and took her hand, kissing her palm. "Are you feeling better?"

She nodded. "I think so. I felt feverish when I awoke, but I feel better now."

"Come here." He pulled her to him in a comforting embrace. Feeling her abdomen, he asked, "Do you think our baby is well?"

"He's been a bit still, but I'm sure he's fine. My mother says babies are stronger than we think." She snuggled close to Gideon's chest and ran her fingers through his beard— what there was of it. "Do you suppose your beard will thicken up as you get older?"

"My father says it will. His was thin and scraggly like mine when he was young."

"It may be thin, but it's not scraggly. You keep it neat and trimmed. Judah's is scraggly."

Gideon let go of Zahava and sat up, rubbing his chin. "Yes, my brother's beard is pretty sparse and thin, that's for sure. But he's still young as well. Not much older than I." He leaned over and kissed her on the forehead. He touched her cheek. "Your skin feels clammy. Are you sure you're better?"

"Mm." She nodded and gathered the blanket around her shoulders. "I had the dream again."

Gideon rose from the bed and reached for his robe hanging on a wall peg. "It's just a dream. Doesn't mean a thing." He tied his belt around his waist and picked up a water pitcher from a table beside the bed. "I'll get you some milk."

Zahava made a face. "That doesn't sound good at all. I'm sick of goat's milk and barley soup."

He laughed. "I won't tell my mother. She prides herself on making the best barley soup in the village."

"I didn't mean it's not good. I've just had so much of it this week…" Gideon's mother, Yenta, treated her well enough, including making barley soup for her when she felt ill. Moshe, his father, a large man, maintained a quiet dignity about himself and remained rather distant from her. He seemed not to know what to do with a daughter now in the house. Gideon had only brothers.

"Oh, I know. But Mother is convinced it cures all that ails you. So what does sound good to you?"

"Just a little wine…watered down."

"I'll be right back. You stay there and rest."

"Let the servants get it. Stay here with me for a while."

Gideon sat on the edge of their bed, turning the clay pitcher round in his hands. He chucked her beneath her chin. "I need to get going. It's my morning to open the shop."

"No, stay. I've grown too accustomed to having you with me all the time this year following our wedding." She pulled him down to her and kissed him. He returned the kiss—long, hard and passionate, lingering. Zahava felt her breath quickening as she leaned into him. She whispered in his ear as she pulled his robe off his shoulders. "Stay with me today."

He groaned, opened his eyes, and sat up. "You *are* feeling better."

Patting the bed, she smiled at him. "I hate it that you have to leave every morning."

Gideon stood, grinning down at her. "But I always come back. And what man wouldn't want to come home to this?"

He tossed the pitcher in the air and caught it, laughing at Zahava's gasp. "I'll send Hasina back with some wine for you."

"Very well." Zahava pursed her lips in a mocking pout. "Go on. Leave your poor, sick wife, heavy with your baby, pining away for you. Perhaps that's all that is wrong with me. I'm simply lovesick for my husband."

"You wouldn't be trying to make me feel guilty, now would you?" Gideon returned to the bedside and touched her arm. "You are the love of my life. You know that."

His touch sent shivers down her back. She covered his hand with her own. "I'm being childish. Go in peace, my husband—I shall await your return this evening."

He pecked her on the cheek and then stood. "That, my dear, I shall look forward to now that you seem on the road to recovery." He touched his heart as he left the room—their personal sign of affection to each other. She touched hers in return, smiling as she gathered the blanket around her and lay back on the luxurious pillows. Closing her eyes, she quickly drifted back to sleep. *11*

The increasing pain in her lower back clawed at the edges of her slumber. "Uhh!" She thought she was dreaming about having her baby. Sitting up, she rubbed her belly. It felt hard. Brilliant rays of the mid-morning sun intruding through the archways of the room stabbed at her eyes like the pain that stabbed at her abdomen. She swung her legs over the edge of the bed and reached for the pitcher of wine, untouched on the bedside table. The wine splashed over the goblet as vise-like fingers gripped her abdomen and sent her to her knees.

chapter 2

The hurried shuffle of footsteps surrounded Zahava, and she felt herself being lifted back into bed. Words reached her through a mist of half consciousness—*midwife, water, too much blood, hurry, Gideon, Hasina, too soon, birthing stool, Lois.* Why were they calling for her mother?

And the pain—increasing, hard, pushing from her body against her will. *Stop!* It was too early.

Hasina and Lois lifted her onto the birthing stool. Through the numbing semi-consciousness she knew her baby had come prematurely. No breaking into the stuffy air of a baby's cry. Only silence and more shuffling of feet. Back onto the bed. Gideon kneeling beside her, weeping. Not touching her. Why wasn't he holding her? Touching her? Unclean. She would be unclean now for…how many days? Was it a boy or a girl?

Blood. And more blood.

"Zahava. Zahava." She forced her eyes open at the sound of her mother's voice. Lois placed a cool cloth on her forehead. "That's right, my child. Awaken."

"My baby? Where is my baby?" She felt around on the bed. "Mother? What did we have?"

Lois turned her head and avoided her daughter's eyes. Dipping the cloth into a basin of water, her soft voice, barely discernible, spoke the words Zahava feared. "You had a boy, but…" She placed the cloth again on Zahava's forehead.

She pushed the cloth and her mother's hand from her face and sat up. "But what? Where is he? Where is my baby?"

Lois sat on the bed and took Zahava's hands into her roughened ones. Her gaze, reflecting pools of painful experience, held her daughter with compassion. "He was born too early, my sweet baby. Too small. He never took a breath."

"Where is he? I want to see him!" Zahava pushed the covers back and struggled to get out of bed. The room swam, and her knees buckled as yellow lights danced in front of her eyes. Darkness threatened to envelop her as Lois gently steered the young woman back to the bed.

"Be careful. You are weak from losing too much blood. You need to rest."

Zahava reached for her mother and pulled the older woman to her. Lois wrapped her arms around her and held her as wrenching sobs sent her body into spasms. "M–my baby is dead? I never even got to hold him." She untangled herself from her mother's embrace and looked at her arms, barely able to talk between sobs. "Empty. N–no baby in my arms. They were supposed to be holding my b–baby, but they are empty. How could this have happened?" Tearing at her robe, she wailed. "My breasts will be swollen with milk, but I have no baby to nurse them. Aghh!" Her moans echoed throughout the house as Lois rocked her back and forth on the bed.

Gideon appeared at the door, his arms dangling helpless at his side. He paced and glanced at Zahava and her mother but, constrained by the Law, could not go to her to comfort her. She was unclean and would be for seven days. The young woman looked at her husband, pleading with her eyes, as he touched his hand to his heart, tears streaming down his cheeks. She touched a trembling hand to her own heart and passed into unconsciousness again.

On the evening of the fifteenth day, Zahava stood before the *mikveh* with her mother. The self-examination had been performed, and she was found to have ceased bleeding. She handed Lois her jewelry, let down her hair, and recited the blessing: *Who has sanctified us with his commandments and commanded us on immersion.* The rough stone on the edge of the *mikveh* steps gave her traction as she descended into the soothing, cleansing waters. Still weak, her knees trembled as she immersed herself completely, letting the holy water swirl around her and bring with it a blessed sense of purification. She pulled her hair about her shoulders as the dark tresses floated around her. Every portion of her body must be submerged for the cleansing to be complete. She closed her eyes, recited the blessing once more, then immersed herself again.

She left the waters feeling at least a portion of her sorrows washed away. Her mother handed Zahava drying towels and assisted her in dressing to go meet Gideon. She could be with her husband, feel his warm assuring embrace, rest in his strength.

Zahava sat on a chair before a small table in her room and watched Hasina fuss over the meal. "Hasina, I am grateful for your attention to every detail—just the right placement, the correct amount. I am not inclined to such precision."

The Egyptian servant smiled and ducked her head. Clutter did not bother Zahava. Clean-up was always something which, in her thinking, could be done later.

She was no longer *niddah.* She could touch her husband, not simply see him from across the room. She could kiss him, caress him, run her fingers through his hair.

Hasina hurried out of the room. Zahava wandered from one end of their quarters to the other, waiting for Gideon to appear.

Although their baby did not live until the eighth day to be circumcised and named, in her mind she called him David, after King David. Her arms ached for the baby that came in pain and left without so much as a kiss from his mother. She folded her arms over breasts tender and heavy with milk that her child would never suckle and rubbed the binding wrapped around her to encourage the milk to dissipate. Approaching the bronze mirror, she rearranged her hair, still damp from the *mikveh*. Should she pull her braid over her shoulder or let it hang down the back? She liked it over her shoulder. Surprised at her feelings of timidity at being with Gideon again, she paced. Oh, they had conversed some, but it was awkward. No intimacy allowed.

Hasina had brought a tray of fruit and cheese as per Zahava's instructions. Gideon's favorites—mangos, grapes, and goat cheese. And wine, of course, and bread. She heard something at the entrance and whirled around to see Gideon standing in the archway to their room, a sheepish grin on his face. He held a small parcel in his hand and touched his hand to his heart.

All shyness and hesitancy left Zahava the moment she saw him. With a small squeal of excitement she ran to his arms and covered his face with kisses. "Oh, I've missed you so much, my dear husband. Seeing you and talking to you but not being able to touch you has been torture for me."

Gideon set the parcel on the table and enveloped her in his arms. "Shh, shh. For me too. I longed to hold you and comfort you and…" He tried to swallow a sob, but the agony of losing their son leapt from his soul, and he wept, his moans mingling with hers.

"Oh, Gideon, our baby, our ba–baby boy." Zahava buried her face in her husband's shoulder and wept with him. Hot tears stung her eyes and wet his robe. She was back in her husband's arms and could let her emotions flow at their will. They clung to each other, crumpling to the floor in their anguish. Finally, their weeping quieted, and they sat in silence on the floor in each other's arms, no desire to move—content to rest in the security of their embrace.

Gideon sighed. "We can have more children. We will never forget him, our firstborn, but we can have more."

"I have been calling him David. He's my little David."

"Very well, David it shall be." Gideon stood and picked up the forgotten parcel from the table. "I brought you a gift."

"How thoughtful, Gideon. But you are gift enough to me."

"And you to me, but these came in on our latest shipment from Egypt, and they reminded me of you."

She winced as Gideon helped her stand.

"Are you in pain? Did I hurt you?" Gideon cradled her elbow to steady her. "This has been too much for you. Come, sit down." He led her to a chair beside the table.

"I am recovering well, but I am still in some pain. The milk…" She ducked her head and felt the heat rise to her cheeks.

"It is painful for you? The milk?"

"Y–yes…I am engorged and swollen, but the midwives say the bindings will help keep the swelling down and prevent more milk from forming."

"I had no idea."

Zahava wiped her eyes with the edge of her sleeve and, still sniffling, untied the ribbons around the package. A heavy gold bracelet clanked as she pulled it out of the fabric in which it was wrapped. "Oh! How beautiful, Gideon." Atop the cuff of gold in a carved setting rested a large jade stone, glinting at her in the soft light. She wrapped it around her wrist immediately. "This is extravagant. You spoil me." She smiled and kissed her husband's cheek. "But I love being spoiled."

Gideon picked up the fabric wrapping. "There's more. Where are they?" He shook out the packaging, and a pair of matching earrings fell out on the table—large dangling hoops with stones of jade embedded in the edges of the circles.

Zahava giggled with excitement. She removed the small gold earrings she wore and inserted the large hoops. "How exquisite." She looked up at her husband and tilted her head.

"The jade stones match your eyes, your beautiful eyes."

Hasina approached the entrance and, upon seeing they had not eaten yet, backed away. A small smile flitted at the corners of her mouth. Zahava beckoned the servant to come and serve them. Hasina moved quietly and unobtrusively into the room and poured goblets of wine for them before she exited.

Zahava looked at the stricken expression on her husband's face. She desired him, yet the thought of encouraging relations with him made her uneasy. Her body had changed. Would he feel the same about her? She feared he would not. She was not only fearful and timid physically, but emotionally. How would she feel welcoming him into her body, knowing that the seed he deposited in her womb could cause such heartache? Her hands trembled as she held her wine.

"Zahava, you're trembling."

"I'm just weak from losing so much blood." She set her goblet down. "I think I need to rest for a minute."

Gideon led her to their bed and helped her lie down. He sat on the edge of the mattress watching her. He started to remove the bracelet.

She pulled her wrist out of his grasp. "No, my dearest. I don't want to take it off. I just need to close my eyes for a moment, then we shall eat." She caressed his arm. "Come lie beside me and hold me." Gideon eased himself down beside her and gently encircled her in his arms. She snuggled into his chest and took a deep breath. "I love the scent of you."

"Umm, and I you." He stroked her hair and fingered the large hoop earring. "Rest, my love. Just rest."

She woke sometime later—how long she'd been asleep she did not know. Feeling the bedclothes beside her, she realized she was in bed by herself. She sat up, her heart banging against her chest. "Gideon? Gideon. Where are you?"

"I'm here, my love." She could see his shadow against the recessed window in the archway overlooking the courtyard. He walked to the bed. "You fell asleep."

Zahava patted the cover beside her. "I'm sorry. Come back to bed. Hold me in your arms. I long for you."

Gideon carefully lowered himself once more into the bed beside his wife. "I…I don't want to hurt you."

"You won't, but I must have you once again." She ran her hands over his chest and kissed his bronze skin. His body responded to accommodate her desire for him.

He leaned up on one elbow and touched her cheek. "Zahava, are you sure it's not too soon? I'm willing to wait."

"The Law says seven days, and it's been over seven days. I'm fearful to wait longer…fearful that I will start to avoid you. Fearful of myself, not you." She sighed and whispered in his ear, moving closer into his body, "Come and take me, my husband. Now. Take me now."

chapter 3

Zahava knew immediately. Knew as only a woman can that she was once again with child. The two months since they lost little David had passed agonizingly slowly. Phantom cries of a baby at night. No infant to nurse at her breasts. She longed to have another child right away, longed to fill her empty arms. Hadn't her mother had baby after baby? And she was fine. One of her brothers was born just barely nine months after his older sister. That meant Lois had conceived during her days of purification. Zahava smiled thinking how she saw her mother in a different light since she was a wife herself now.

Gideon didn't know yet. She would tell him tonight. She fingered the gold and jade earrings that had become a constant adornment for her. The refined gold reflected the joy of their love and the somber green of the jade the sorrow of losing their child. She'd selected a rich-toned brown robe and a gold head covering, trimmed in a woven tapestry of greens, golds, and turquoises. The jewelry set the outfit off perfectly. She wanted to look special when she told her husband that they were expecting another child.

"What? You are with child again—so soon?" Gideon's brow crinkled the way it did in a curious blend of bewilderment and displeasure. She never knew which it was.

Tears stung her eyes. "I thought you would be excited at the prospect of having another baby." Gideon reached for her, but she pulled away from him as she brushed the moisture from her eyelid with the tip of her finger. "You did have something to do with this, you know."

He folded his arms and walked through the archway onto the balcony. The sun's rays painted brilliant yellows and oranges across the evening sky and lit up the bronze in his skin. He spoke without turning to face her. "I'm not displeased, Zahava. You've misunderstood me. My concern is for you—your well-being." He came back into the room. "Have you regained enough strength to carry another child?" He shifted his weight and popped his knuckles in that annoying habit of his. "I…I want a child—desperately—but I don't want to lose you. I…" Emotion caught in his throat and cut off his sentence.

"Oh, Gideon." Zahava reached for his hand and allowed him to embrace her. "I feel strong and ready to have another baby."

He held her tight in his arms. "I don't know what I would do if I lost you. Please, please take care of yourself." He pushed back from her and looked into her eyes. "Are you feeling well? Does everything seem to be in order?"

She laughed and kissed his hand. "I am fine, except when you insist on popping your knuckles. It sets my teeth on edge."

A chuckle escaped his lips as he flexed his fingers. "I suppose I'm nervous."

"With me? I'm your wife, and we love each other dearly. As long as we have each other, all is well."

All was not well. Zahava recalled their conversation many times after nearly losing this second baby after only four months. She battled premature cramping and spotting of blood—precursors of threatening labor—the ensuing months of carrying the child. The physicians ordered her to bed for the remainder of her time.

But at last she managed to bring their son into the world—small but healthy.

Zahava stroked his red, wrinkled cheek as she put him to her breast to suckle. Her mother-in-law reached for the tiny bundle and sputtered. "The wet nurse awaits the child."

Zahava tightened her hold on the infant and glared at Yenta. "No wet nurse will feed my baby. My son will nurse at his mother's breast."

Her mother-in-law's mouth set in a grim line as she folded her hands. "But all of our sons were tended by a wet nurse. It is our custom." She forced a slight smile. "That will free you to regain your strength quicker to service your husband."

"My breasts were heavy with milk and ached for the child we lost. I will not ache unnecessarily for a living child." The prestige of having a wet nurse for her son would not preempt her from taking care of her own child.

Yenta turned on her heel and strode out of the room as Lois fussed about Zahava, straightening the room, cooing over the child, trying to ignore Yenta. Gideon stood in the archway of their quarters, grinning and craning his neck to catch a glimpse of his son. Zahava smiled at him and, breaking the suction from her breast with her finger, gave the child to Lois to take to his father.

He looked at Lois with eyes wide. "He's so small." Touching the blanket with his fingertips, he pulled his hand back quickly as the baby let out a lusty cry. "Is he well? Will he…will he live?"

Lois chuckled. "With a bellow like that, I believe he is fine."

Gideon's eyes filled with moisture as he looked across the room at his wife. "We have a son, my love. We have a son." Lois handed the baby to him. He held him clumsily, the child barely big enough to cover one of his father's hands. "I'm afraid I'll drop him."

The infant stopped his fussing and blinked his eyes at Gideon.

"Looks like you have the magic touch." Lois left the baby with Gideon and returned to Zahava's bedside.

Spent and weak after hours of labor, Zahava closed her eyes. They had a son. She smiled. She wanted to sleep, but the pain of the tearing from the birth was too much to allow her to relax. Searing pain shot through her body every time she moved. She was not comfortable lying on her back or her side.

The midwife kneaded her stomach to expel the afterbirth, eliciting moans from Zahava.

Gideon handed the baby to a servant and motioned to Lois. "What is she doing? She's hurting Zahava." He took a step toward the interior of the room.

Lois laughed. "That's why men need not be admitted to the birthing room." She waved her hand. "Shoo, get out of here. She's fine. We are taking good care of her." She looked down the passageway from the quarters. "I think you probably need to go to your mother and assure her that you and Zahava agree about the wet nurse situation."

"Yes, I shall do that. You're certain Zahava is going to be—"

"Perfectly fine. Now, off with you." Gideon handed the baby back to Lois and, after a final kiss on the little one's head, left the room.

On the eighth day the boy was circumcised and named Caleb. But he was sickly. He would nurse hungrily, then vomit violently. He grew weaker and weaker daily until Zahava could not coax him to nurse at all.

"Come on, Caleb." She tweaked his cheek. "You must eat."

He turned his face from side to side against her breast, not even strong enough to grab the nipple and suckle. Finally, he grew limp in her arms and exhaled a final soft breath.

"Noo!" Her screams echoed through the house.

Gideon dashed up the stairs, drawn by Zahava's cries, and grabbed the child from her arms. "Breathe, son, breathe!"

Lois and Yenta stood helplessly by as they frantically flailed around for anything that would bring their son back—cold water in his face, swinging him, breathing into his mouth. But the boy was gone. At only a few weeks old, he was gone.

chapter 4

Zahava conceived quickly again but miscarried that one early—just two months along.

After that, she carried a child to term that was stillborn.

Two more early miscarriages followed.

Zahava felt something rupture deep in her womb with the last one, and the hemorrhaging was profuse—bright red blood that flowed like a river from her body. After days of bleeding, it finally slowed, but it would not stop completely. Every morning it was the same thing.

She stared at soiled linen that screamed evidence that her body was diseased. This had gone on far too long now. She'd not had a "white day" for months—lonely, isolated months. Zahava's days were long and boring.

She rang for Hasina. The servant appeared quickly, and Zahava stared at the woman. For the first time, Zahava became aware of what a beautiful, mature woman her servant was. She wore a white sarong, trimmed in gold, belted with a gold sash. Her dark, straight hair hung to her shoulders and was caught up with a gold band around her forehead. The only jewelry she ever wore were slender gold earrings that reached almost to her shoulders—soft, shimmery slivers.

Zahava knew very little about this woman who tended to her every need. "Hasina, have you never married and had children?"

Hasina startled and looked down at her hands.

"I don't mean to intrude. I simply realized a beautiful woman like you should have a husband and a family, but I've never heard you mention them. And you live here with us. Obviously you are not married."

Hasina stood rooted to the spot where she entered. "I..."

"It is fine, Hasina. You may speak." Zahava's state of uncleanness had separated her from the family for months. Although they conversed with her from a distance concerning household matters, gradually they gave up trying to carry on any kind of meaningful conversation. Even Gideon. It simply had become too painful for him to see her often. She was lonely for someone to talk to. Hasina, being a pagan, did not have the same restrictions.

The servant shuffled her feet. "I...I had a husband at one time, but he was taken to Rome. I don't know where he is now."

"Children?"

"A son was born to us, but he died in a fire when he was just a baby. Then I was with child again. When my husband was taken away, I lost it...shortly before your husband's family brought me to this land." Hasina held her hands tightly in front of her as if doing so would shield her heart from the recalled pain.

"Oh, I am so sorry, Hasina. I never knew."

"It was a long time ago. Your family treats me well."

"So you can understand the agony I am experiencing?"

"I think I do." She dropped her gaze, still standing in front of Zahava. "A mother's pain is the same when any child is lost, no matter the race or the color of the skin." She flicked a tear from her cheek. "I am sorry for your pain."

Zahava sighed and held her stained bedclothes out toward the woman.

Hasina took the soiled linens and hurried out of the room and down the stairs.

Weeks, months passed, but the issue of blood continued. Zahava's quarters were all but quarantined. Lois would come to see her during the days when she was *niddah,* and some of the other women. But other than that, she was alone except for Hasina. The servant became her constant companion.

Every morning Zahava arose and checked to see if perhaps during the night the bleeding had ceased…only to be disappointed once again. Or if perhaps the flow might cease for a day or two, the wretched fluid would appear again before she could be declared clean.

Hasina appeared with Zahava's breakfast. She did not speak but raised her eyebrows to Zahava's shaking of her head. She arranged the fruit, cheese and bread on the tray and stepped back, hesitating, not rushing off to tend to her duties as she usually did.

"What is it, Hasina?" Zahava paused and swung her legs over the bed. "I think I'd like to get up and wash before I eat."

The servant watched as Zahava arose and covered the stained linens over with a coverlet.

Hasina poured water from a ewer into the basin on Zahava's vanity. "May it please my mistress…" She removed Zahava's nightclothes from her and let them drop to the floor as Zahava sat at the vanity. Hasina wrung the cool water from a sponge and wiped her arms and back.

"You have something you'd like to say to me? You know you are free to speak."

Hasina took a deep breath. She rinsed the sponge out

again and handed it to Zahava to do her more personal cleansing. Hasina averted her eyes. "Would my mistress be…?" Her voice, low and soft, heavy with her accent, was unsure.

Zahava handed the sponge back to Hasina, who discarded it and got a clean one. "Be what? Upset? Angry?"

Hasina shook her head. "No. What's the word…willing? May I be so bold to ask whether my mistress would be willing to consider some of the ancient remedies from my country to attempt to heal…to stop the…?" She ducked her head. "I dare not presume upon you. I simply…"

Zahava stared at her servant. *This woman truly cares about me. She was willing to risk her position or chastisement to suggest this.* "Oh, Hasina. You need not be hesitant to express your concern."

"I know something about the ancient healing arts from my country. Would you like to try…?" The woman couldn't seem to get the words out.

"I don't know. I cannot go against what Torah teaches."

"Of course." Hasina fell silent. She gathered up the bed linens and walked toward the stairs.

"Wait. What were you about to say?"

Hasina turned to her mistress. "Please. I mean no disrespect. You have been to your priest to pray for you?"

"Yes."

"And still the discharge continues."

"You know better than anyone else that it does." Zahava pulled a clean robe around her shoulders and stood. "It has been two years now since the last miscarriage, and still I bleed. If I count the bleeding from those as well, and after Caleb, it has been four years that I have been *niddah*—more than I have been clean."

"I simply thought that perhaps you might be willing to try something else."

hopeless

Zahava's hands trembled as she belted her robe. Images of magicians, conjuring, and amulets danced in her head—things strictly forbidden to her people. But she was desperate. She stared at Hasina. "What are you suggesting?"

chapter 5

Hasina dropped the linens on the floor and walked toward Zahava. "Nothing offensive. Something simple." She stopped a few feet from her mistress and folded her hands. "Our physicians always thoroughly cleanse the outer body, including shaving the whole body."

Zahava put her hand on the top of her head. "My hair? No, that's not possible."

Hasina smiled. "No, not your head, but everyplace else."

Zahava's eyes widened. "Everyplace else?"

"Yes."

"I don't know. What would Gideon think? I don't want to displease him." She looked down. "And it sounds embarrassing."

The Egyptian shook her head. "How would he even know? He hasn't come near you intimately in months, since the last pregnancy. It will grow back quickly. And you wouldn't have to go to a physician. I could do it for you." Her voice gained confidence with each sentence.

"Shaving all hair from the body? That's all?"

"No, I would make a poultice of acacia leaves and place it on your abdomen." Hasina looked at Zahava and raised her eyebrows with a reassuring nod of her head. "That's all."

"No conjuring or amulets?"

"Nothing like that."

Zahava took a deep breath. "I'm frightened, Hasina. I dare not do anything to displease my husband or Jehovah God by seeking healing from a source that is forbidden."

"Don't you think your God would want you to be well? He does not forbid healing, does he?"

"Well, no, but our Law has very strict instructions about what to do and not to do about a…a condition such as mine."

"And you have followed those instructions, have you not?"

"As closely as I can."

"Do you think your God would be angry to try something else that is not specifically forbidden?"

Zahava sat down once again at her vanity and held her head in her hands. She swallowed the sobs she felt mounting in her throat and turned her head from side to side. "I don't know—I don't know. I have no answers to any of this." Zahava stood and walked to the balcony. Raising her face to the warmth of the rising sun, she closed her eyes and filled her chest with as much of the pristine morning air as she could. A slight breeze ruffled her hair.

Tomorrow was Yom Kippur. This evening the family would be gathering for a family meal and a time of prayer and repentance before entering into the fast. Would they permit her to at least participate from a distance? She caught her breath in a sob that surprised her. She was so lonely. She ached to feel Gideon's arms around her. Why was she cursed to bear this sickness? What had she done to deserve this?

She turned to Hasina. "After Yom Kippur, we'll discuss this matter further." She dismissed her servant with a wave of her hand. "After Yom Kippur."

Lois entered Zahava's quarters, calling to her. She balanced Zahava's newest sibling, James, on her hip. Zahava let out a laugh and opened her arms wide for her youngest brother.

"My, how big you are! Come here and let me see your muscles."

The child stuck his thumb in his mouth and laid his head on his mother's shoulder. He stared at Zahava through thick, dark eyelashes. Lois tweaked his cheek. "Now, shame on you, James. Don't you be shy with your own sister." She set the toddler down on the floor, pushing him toward Zahava's open arms. But the boy whimpered as he resisted and clung to his mother's robe. "Oh, pshaw. You're being silly. Stop it."

Zahava reached down and picked him up. "Come here, little one." The child pushed against her and stretched his arms toward his mother. "Ma-a-a-ma!" The wail pierced through the room as well as Zahava's heart. No child had ever turned away from her. Now her own brother didn't want to be around her. She returned him to Lois and turned away from them.

Lois quieted the child with one of her bracelets and set him on the floor to play with it. "He's just a child, Zahava, and he's not been around you that much. He doesn't know you." Lois pulled her daughter into her arms in a smothering embrace and held her.

Zahava nestled into Lois's familiar cuddle. "I know, Mother. I'm so lonely, and the touch of an embrace…"

"So I guess I don't have to ask if you are still… experiencing your problem."

"I don't understand why Jehovah God has put this on me. You have babies like it's nothing more than a slight diversion from your daily routine, and this…this has become the all-consuming focus for us." She took the tip of her sleeve and wiped her eyes. "I've cried until I think surely I have no more tears. Then I cry all the more. I miss Gideon. Why must I bear this alone? Why does the Law take my husband away from me when I need him the most?"

She sat on the edge of her bed. "I feel so guilty, but I don't know what I'm guilty of. I don't know what to repent for. What have I done to deserve this?"

Lois sat next to her and clasped both of her hands in her own. "Oh, my precious child. I cannot answer your questions. My heart hurts with you. You know when your child hurts, as a mother, you hurt as well. It doesn't matter how old the child is." She brushed Zahava's hair out of her eyes. "You look like you did when you were a little girl and cried over a scraped knee."

"This is a more than a scraped knee, Mother." Zahava drew a handkerchief from her robe and blew her nose.

"I didn't mean to belittle your pain." She patted her daughter's knee. "Although I have no answers for you, I do know that God is good, and he will answer your prayers."

"When? We've prayed and prayed, but he seems to turn a deaf ear to us. The priest just says to pray and be faithful, but nothing is happening to make me better. I have no clean days anymore. It all appears to be hopeless."

"It is never hopeless with God. Our father Abraham—"

"I know, I know, Mother." Zahava rolled her eyes and sighed. "Abraham and Sarah had Isaac in their old age and fathered our nation. But I'm not Sarah, and Gideon is not Abraham. God has not come to us with a promise to father a nation. At this point, even to be with my husband is impossible. How can I have children when I cannot even touch my husband without making him unclean?"

"Nothing is impossible with God."

Zahava fell silent. It was of no use to argue with her mother. Lois loved her dearly, but Zahava didn't want to hear the platitudes of how good God was when all she knew at the moment was the evidence of a barren womb and illness. If God loved her, why was he subjecting her to months and years of misery? She shook her head. She didn't want to think about God anymore.

Lois gathered James in her arms. "Come, little one. We must get back home."

"Mother, I didn't mean to speak unkindly."

Lois touched Zahava on the shoulder. "I know. I don't know how I would feel in your position. But keep on trusting God. He will make a way for you. You'll see. Your father and I are praying for you—every day. Something will come along."

Something will come along. Maybe it already had. Hasina's proposal seemed more appealing and plausible as Zahava thought about it. Perhaps she would consider it. What could it hurt? Yes, perhaps she would consider it after all.

chapter 6

Zahava arrived early and carried her own chair. She took her place apart from the family for the eve of Yom Kippur celebration. Gideon was nowhere to be seen. Choosing a place partially hidden by tapestry hangings, but where she could still observe, she placed her chair and sat down. She needed to be particularly certain tonight that no one be contaminated by touching her or anything that belonged to her. In doing so that person would become unclean and unable to participate in the festivities.

The women hustled about finishing up the preparations as Gideon's brothers and families trickled in. Wives and babies had been added through the years and the chatter of a family gathering filled the air. There he was. Gideon scanned the room as he came through the entry, his eyes searching each face, then he smiled when he spotted her. He left his brother's side immediately and hurried toward her. He stopped at the prescribed distance from her and touched his hand to his heart. "My beloved, I've missed you so. Are you…are you well?"

She thought her heart was going to leap out of her throat as she rose and touched her hand to her chest as well. Her arms ached to reach out and embrace him and cover his face with kisses, but she could not. She dropped her head and shook it.

"Zahava, look at me."

She peered up at her handsome husband through tear-heavy eyes.

"Please do not be discouraged. We will find a way through this. God will not abandon us to this fate. Listen—"

Zahava shook her head. "You are going to get tired of waiting for me. You are a virile young man and need your wife. I am no good to you."

"God put us together for a reason. He will not—"

"For what reason? God told our forefathers to be fruitful and multiply. I've not been able to do that. You'd be better off to divorce me and find another wife. The Law allows it. I am no good to you."

"I do not want another wife. I want you. I've heard of—"

"What? More prayers. Another physician? Nobody has been able to help."

Gideon stepped toward her. "Would you quit interrupting and listen to me, please? I love you. I will not leave you. I've heard of a physician in Jerusalem who has treated maladies such as yours successfully. I want to take you to him."

"I'm weary of going to physicians. And the expense—how long can we continue to afford the physicians?"

"As long as it takes."

Gideon's father called the family to the celebration table. Gideon reached his arm out to Zahava, and she shrank from him with alarm. "Don't. Don't touch me."

Moshe looked their way, his face twisted into a scowl.

Zahava shooed him away with a wave of her hand. "You must not defile yourself before Yom Kippur. Go."

"We will discuss this later. I will come to your room after Yom Kippur." He touched his hand to his heart. "You are the one God has given to me, and I will love you eternally." He turned to join his brothers and their families.

The traditional rituals stirred her spirit and made her

heartsick to join in. She repented of every sin she could think of that perhaps she had committed. And then some. *Why God? Why? How long is this going to go on? I simply want to be a wife and mother. Why have I been denied that privilege? What have I done?*

Zahava got out of bed the morning after Yom Kippur and in a fit of rage yanked the bed linens off. "Arrgghh! I am sick unto death of this!" She threw them at the entry just as Hasina entered with her breakfast tray. Hasina flinched and stepped aside as air caught in the fabric.

The bed clothes fluttered harmlessly to the floor. Zahava pressed her hand to her mouth. "Oh! Hasina. I'm sorry."

The servant scooted the linens into a pile with her foot.

"Put the tray down on my vanity table, please." Zahava sat down and selected a slice of orange. "I've thought about your suggestion. Thought much about it."

Hasina raised her eyebrows. "Yes?"

"Gideon told me last night he's heard about a doctor in Jerusalem who he thinks might be able to help me. I need to explore that possibility first."

"Of course." Hasina's expression clouded over. She turned away and picked up the linens.

"That doesn't mean I don't appreciate your concern."

"Yes, I know."

"If this doctor is unable to cure my affliction, I think I might be open to try your treatment. It certainly seems innocuous enough. Who knows, but perhaps something that simple will cure it."

"I sincerely pray the doctor in Jerusalem will prove to

be of help." Hasina turned and left the room, her arms filled with the soiled linens.

That evening Gideon leaned against the archway entrance to Zahava's quarters. "I want to make a side trip to Cana and Nazareth on the way to Jerusalem—business."

Zahava groaned as Gideon explained the details of their trip. "That's going to make a long trip even longer."

"Only by a day or two. It's a perfect time to check on a couple of things. I want to take some products to our vendors in Cana, and there's a wood worker in Nazareth I've heard about who puts out beautiful work. I want to see his products for myself."

Without looking at him Zahava remained seated at her vanity table. "Very well. I don't suppose a few days more will make that much difference."

"Look at me, Zahava."

She turned toward him, her eyes dry but with a lump forming in her throat. *I will not cry. I've cried way too many tears already. I will not let him see me cry anymore.*

"Please don't despair. We will find a cure. I won't stop until we do."

She sighed. "What if there is no cure for my ailment? What if I am cursed to live with this my whole life? You cannot be saddled with a wife you cannot touch or know intimately. You need to—" The lump turned into a sob that interrupted her sentence.

She put her head down on her arms, her shoulders heaving with emotion that racked her entire body. Her sobs escaped as pitiful whimpers. She felt Gideon's hands on her shoulders as he knelt beside her.

Pushing back in horror from him, she stood, the chair clattering to the floor. "No! You mustn't touch me. You'll be un-unclean." Her voice was muffled as Gideon gathered her in his arms.

"I don't care. Oh, God, forgive me, but I don't care. I cannot stand seeing you tortured like this. The illness is bad enough, but to see you isolated from us, pining away here in your quarters—it's simply too cruel. The Law is cruel."

"Don't talk like that, Gideon. You will be ostracized as well. Go. Leave me."

"I'm already tainted from touching you." He tilted her chin up toward his face and kissed her hungrily.

She offered weak resistance, but his embrace drew her in and melted away any feigned opposition. She inhaled the fragrance of his masculinity—a mixture of leather and the sandalwood oil he used in his hair. Her starved emotions responded to his touch. She closed her eyes and leaned into him, relishing in the security of the strength in his body. To feel him touch her in the many familiar patterns they had developed during their marriage sent desire swirling through her veins like warm water. Wrapping her arms around his shoulders she pulled him closer.

He nuzzled her neck, and she let her robe slip down from her shoulders as he covered her chest with soft kisses. "Zahava, Zahava, my beautiful one." His voice had grown husky with passion. Gathering her in his arms, he carried her to their bed, where they were husband and wife once again.

Guilt rushed in with the sunlight that flooded the room the next morning. Zahava stretched and leaned up on her elbow to look at her husband. "This is the way I desire to awaken every morning—watching you wake from your sleep. Even listening to you snore."

He chuckled. "Was I snoring?"

"Just a little." She touched his beard. "You must go to the priest and confess."

Gideon kissed her cheek and swung his legs over the edge of the bed. "I will be *karat*—cut off." Reaching for his robe, he stood and gathered the robe around him. "Perhaps the priest will have mercy on me and only impose the consequences temporarily." He turned and smiled at Zahava over his shoulder as he tied his belt. "These are definitely extenuating circumstances."

She sat up, clutching the bedclothes around her. "Gideon, I…"

"Don't." His smile turned somber as he slipped into his sandals. "Whatever the penalty I must pay, I would do it again. I cannot stand being away from you. Every moment last night with you was worth it."

The priest's judgment was lenient, but Gideon had to stay away from Temple for a period of time, bring a sacrifice and then immerse in the *mikveh*. Zahava stood at the archway and watched Gideon leave and go down the stairs from her quarters. He'd kept a safe distance between them as he reported to her. His pained expression tugged at Zahava's heart strings, but he said what he needed to say and left quickly.

"Gideon." She started down the stairs after him, but he didn't hear her as he left the courtyard. The sound of angry voices from the inside of the house halted her progress. She leaned against the wall, pressing her body against the rough stone. Yenta's shrill screeching tore through the air. "Moshe, you must talk to Gideon—immediately! He must consider divorcing this woman. She can be no wife to him, cannot bear children for him. He will continue to be in trouble, be *karat*. It's time for Gideon to think about finding a new wife."

A dagger pierced through Zahava's heart. She slumped on the stairs, gasping to catch her breath, knowing that Yenta was right. Gideon needed to find a new wife.

chapter 7

Arms folded across his chest, Moshe stood at the entrance of their import/export shop, blocking the door. Gideon knew that stance, knew he was in for a lecture. "Good morning, Father." Gideon stopped in front of him.

"Good morning, son. We need to talk." The large, burly man did not move from the doorway.

Gideon nodded. "Could we go inside?"

Without speaking, Moshe stepped aside and ushered him into the dim shop. Gideon moved a cluster of large clay pots aside and pulled two chairs together. "If those aren't going to sell, we might as well give them to Mother to use in the house."

"I'll do that." Moshe cleared his throat. "We need to talk about your wife. It's been more than years since my grandson was born, and still she bleeds. You have no wife. She is not able to be a true wife to you and meet your needs. In order to have your needs met, you have to transgress the Law. The priest was lenient last time—he may not be inclined to be so again. You need to divorce her." He folded his arms again, this time on his protruding belly.

"She has a name."

"What?"

"My wife has a name. She is not some nameless woman living in the upstairs room of our house. She is Zahava, my beloved. I will not divorce her. I am convinced we will find a cure."

"And if you don't?"

"Even if we don't, I will not abandon her."

"Our patience is wearing thin, son. If she doesn't regain her health soon, you will need to move her out of the house. At least that will lessen the possibility of contamination on every hand. How much money and how much time do you intend to spend on this? If I have to cut off funds from you, I will."

"Cut off funds?" Gideon slammed his fist onto his thigh. "How can you do that? This is our family business. We all share equally."

Moshe shook a stubby finger in Gideon's face. "You keep up this futile search for an elusive cure, and you'll see how I can do that."

"I will not abandon her. I will go wherever we need to go to find a cure." Gideon rose, sending the chair clattering to the floor and left the shop.

Moshe's voice followed him. "You heed what I say. Find a cure quickly or you'll find yourself cast out along with her."

Zahava tried to summon a smile when Gideon turned on his donkey to check on her. Their little caravan of a few beasts carrying merchandise and several servants made its way toward Jerusalem with Zahava and Hasina maintaining a short distance from the rest of the group. Gideon stayed close enough to keep an eye on them, but the journey had been as lonely as her days at the house.

Slowing his donkey down to keep gait with hers, he

leaned toward her. "Are you growing weary?"

Zahava nodded and shifted her weight. "I just pray we find an answer this time."

"We will find a cure, my love. We will continue to look until we do. I don't care how far we have to travel. We'll go to Egypt if we have to."

She shot a look at Hasina, whose face was masked with a veil as she walked beside Zahava's donkey. The edges of the servant's eyes crinkled. She turned her head and looked into the distance.

They approached the small village of Nazareth in the heat of the late afternoon. On their way to set up their tents for the night, Gideon pulled his donkey over at a small house with a workshop off to the side. "This must be it." Several children of varying ages chased one another under a large palm tree. Laughter skittered from child to child as the boys teased the girls who were shoveling dirt into clay vessels.

Zahava followed him and slipped off her donkey, rubbing her hip. "Ah, it feels good to get off that bony back." She smiled as she watched the children. The laughter of children—there was nothing like it. Spotting a well by the workshop, she nodded for Hasina to walk in front of her to clear the way. Glancing from side to side, Zahava walked cautiously behind her servant. The donkeys brayed and stomped their feet. "The donkeys are thirsty too."

Hasina pulled a cup from a bag she had slung over her body and drew water for Zahava as she stood by the side of the well. The cool water sparkled in the bronze cup. It soothed her thirst as it tracked down her dry throat. She wiped her mouth with the tip of her headdress.

As she handed the cup back to Hasina, a young man emerged from the workshop. He set the hammer and chisel he'd held in his hands on a simple wooden bench that sat outside the door of the shop. Weaving his way through the children, touching first one and then another, tousling their hair and speaking a word to them, he picked up a wooden pail and headed in their direction.

Zahava backed up several steps, holding up her hand. The young man looked to be in his early twenties, and he smiled at her, revealing a deep crease in his left cheek, as he lowered the bucket on a rope into the well. Muscles rippled in his strong arms as he retrieved the pail from the depths of the well and carried it past the women to water the donkeys. He refilled the bucket twice before the animals were satisfied.

As the young man replaced the pail, Gideon approached with an older man who held a small, intricately carved chair. "Zahava, look at this beautiful piece." With a sweep of his arm, he introduced her. "This is my wife, Zahava. Zahava, this is Joseph."

The older man, his mouth turned up in a slight smile, nodded. Gideon took the chair from him and turned it upside down. The underside was as smoothly finished as the top. "Don't you think this would sell well? It's lightweight and some of the most exquisite work I've ever seen." He handed the stool back to the man. "You are quite a craftsman."

A full, broad smile spread across the man's face. "Actually, my son makes these. I'm very proud of his work." He looked at the younger man. "This is my son, Jesus."

Jesus grinned and walked toward the group and greeted Gideon. "I'm happy to meet you, sir."

Zahava kept her distance and inched back with each exchange until she was on the other side of the well with Hasina. "Yes, I agree. Beautiful." She only answered Gideon's direct question, her voice quiet and low. She stared at Jesus and his father as they conducted business with Gideon.

Gideon set the chair on the ground. "How many of the chairs do you have?"

Jesus answered, "We have five completed. I'm working on a sixth."

"I'll purchase them all. However, I cannot take them with me. We are on our way to Jerusalem. After we return home to Capernaum, I shall send someone for them." He dug in his bag for money. Coins clinked as he pulled out the leather purse.

Joseph held up his hand. "No need for that. We'll get them ready and hold them for you."

Gideon handed several coins to Joseph. "I insist. Here's a deposit. A workman is worthy of his hire."

"Very well." Joseph took the coins. "Is there anything else you might need?"

Gideon looked at Zahava, then at the donkeys. "Actually there is. I'd like to purchase a carrying chair to make my wife's journey a bit more comfortable. You wouldn't happen to—"

"I have just the thing." The younger man motioned to the shop. "I made one for a customer in the village, but he decided he wanted a larger one for a horse to pull instead of putting it on the back of a donkey. If you think you'd like it, I could fit it to her donkey in the morning and you could be on your way by midday."

"Let's have a look at it." Gideon followed Jesus into the shop. Zahava could hear them chatting, then they emerged with the carrying chair in Jesus's hands. He went to Zahava's donkey and waited as Gideon removed the saddle. The donkey brayed and shook his head. Jesus spoke to the animal and gently eased the carrying chair onto his back. The beast snorted, then grew quiet.

"Here, hold the top of the chair while I see if the straps fit."

Gideon held the chair still as Jesus reached under the donkey and pulled the leather bindings tight. He raised up. "I just need to make the buckles tighter and maybe carve out the underside of the chair a bit more. The better the fit of the chair to the donkey's back, the easier it is for him to carry you."

Gideon ran his hand over the chair. "Even this is a beautiful piece of work. We'll take it."

Joseph joined the two men and indicated an area behind their house shaded by more palms and cedars. "You are welcome to bed your animals down here. Feel free to use the well. And, please, honor us by being our guests for supper in our home."

Gideon looked at Zahava. She lowered her head and shook it ever so slightly. Her heart pounded. *No! I'm unclean. No, Gideon.*

"Thank you for your gracious hospitality. My wife is not well, and she would be more comfortable in our tent."

"Then we shall bring supper to your tent for you to enjoy in privacy."

Gideon nodded. "You are very kind. Thank you." He ran his hand once again over the smooth surface of the chair. "I've been praying for a craftsman such as you to have as a resource for our business. Jehovah has answered my prayers."

Jesus spoke. "Our heavenly Father always answers our prayers when we pray believing." He looked toward the women. "Sometimes he does not answer when we wish he would, but he will answer." He nodded. "He will answer in due time."

chapter 8

Their small party approached the Golden Gate of the great city of Jerusalem in silence. They stared at the immense wall surrounding the city and plodded through the gate. It was the first time Zahava had ever been to Jerusalem for anything other than one of the festivals. Without the jocularity and celebratory spirit of the pilgrims, the city seemed somewhat subdued, although there was plenty of hustle and bustle around the Temple area. Groups of city elders and priests clustered around the gate. Men stood toe to toe, face to face, debating loudly.

Gideon chuckled. "Pharisees arguing with the Sadducees. It never ceases."

"What do they argue about?" Zahava twisted around in the carrying chair and stared as they rode past them.

"Everything. Nothing. They disagree about points of the Law. When Messiah will come. What happens in the hereafter. It doesn't matter. They simply argue." Gideon turned in front of a large, walled-in house and tied his donkey. "This is where we are staying." He rang the bell on the gate in the sandstone wall and an older servant with leathery skin and a solemn countenance answered the summons.

"Menachem is expecting us. I am Gideon, and this is my wife, Zahava. Would you inform him of our arrival, please?"

Bowing slightly at the waist, revealing a bald spot on the top of his head, he spoke. "Yes, please come in. My master awaits you." They stepped from the hot, dusty street resounding with the quarreling voices and the clatter of carts and horses into a lush green oasis brilliant with flowering hibiscus, bougainvillea, and splashing fountains.

A short man with a barrel chest—a business associate of Gideon's family—hurried out the door to greet them. Huffing and perspiring in the heat, he extended his arms. "Welcome, welcome, my friends. We've been expecting you. Please come in."

"Thank you, Menachem. It's good to see you again." Gideon gripped the man's arm in greeting. "We are grateful for your hospitality." He turned to Zahava. "My wife, Zahava. We come seeking help for her from the physician, Tevya. Do you know him?"

Menachem barely sent a glance Zahava's way. He nodded. "He is usually at the gate this time of day. I'll take you over and introduce you after I show you to your quarters." The thick stone walls offered a cool respite from the glaring sun. Zahava, not unaccustomed to elegant surroundings, nevertheless was impressed with Menachem's estate. A small middle-aged woman walked into the room and bowed toward them. Menachem went to her side. "My wife, Esther."

The woman's smile flashed a warm salutation. "Welcome to our home. We are honored to have you."

"Come." Menachem went in front of them up steep marble stairs and ushered them into quarters with several rooms adjoining a circular central area. Archways leading onto a balcony surrounded a small pool. "I trust you will be comfortable here." He summoned servants who brought trays of fruit, wine, and towels, then stood aside to await further orders.

"This is more than adequate. Thank you." Gideon instructed the servants to take his things to the adjoining room, and Hasina took Zahava's to the quarters directly across from Gideon's.

Their hosts left them to settle in.

The couple stood on opposite sides of the turquoise pool after dismissing the servants. Water burbled over rocks into a second pool where water lilies floated and fish darted in and out through the dangling roots of the plants. Zahava sat on the edge of the pool and trailed her fingers through the water. "It's cool. It feels good."

Gideon untied his belt and slipped his outer robe off his shoulders. "I'm going to wash up and go see Rabbi Tevya right away."

"It can wait until tomorrow. I'm tired." Zahava sighed and removed her headdress and outer garment as well.

"No, I want to get this in motion. I won't set it up for you to see him today, but I want to inquire when he has time available for you." *49*

"Do our hosts know the nature of my illness?"

Gideon shook his head. "He only knows you are ill. But when you keep yourself away from us, he will soon guess."

"It's embarrassing."

"We cannot worry about that. He's a kind man, as is his wife."

Zahava stood and pivoted toward her room. She didn't remember when she'd felt so weary. Her legs were so weak she didn't know if they would hold her up until she could get to a bed and lie down. "I believe I'll go rest for a bit."

"Yes, dear, do that." Gideon watched her. "Zahava."

She turned toward him. "Yes?"

"We will find a cure. I don't know when, but we will search until we do." He touched his hand to his chest. "You are the one who has captured my heart."

hopeless

Tears brimmed in Zahava's eyes as she touched her chest. She nodded at Gideon and went to her room.

chapter 9

"Zahava. Zahava, wake up."

She heard Gideon's voice in the distance, through the line of people plodding through the blood on the line drawn across her mind. *The bloody nightmare again. Am I sick? I must be running a fever. Wake up, Zahava, wake up.* She fought to open her eyes. Slipping and sliding through the bloody mess in her dream, she turned from her pursuit of whatever awaited in the distance and gasped, sitting up in the bed. Dark outside. Her heart raced. Perspiration beaded on her face.

Hasina stood over her with a candle, Gideon directly behind her. Gideon moved Hasina aside and sat on the edge of the bed, encircling Zahava in his arms.

"Don't, Gideon. Do–n't." She dissolved into tears. "Now you are unclean too." She shook her head and pulled away from him. "Don't."

He took a wet cloth Hasina handed him and put it on Zahava's forehead. "The dream again?"

She nodded.

"You're burning up with fever. I'm going for the physician."

Too weak to protest, she allowed him to lay her back on the sweat-drenched pillow. "Is it morning or night?"

"It's just daybreak, my love." Gideon turned to Hasina

as he rose. "Tend to this soiled bedding, change her gown, and try to get that fever down. I shall return as soon as I can with the physician."

"Yes, Master. I shall take care of her."

"The journey was too much for her." He slapped his leg in frustration as he strode from the room.

Zahava took the cloth from her forehead and leaned up on her elbow. "It's not your fault. I…" Her voice trailed off as she lay back down, and her eyes fluttered shut. Faintly aware of Hasina changing her night clothes and rolling her from side to side as she changed the bedding beneath her, she wondered in her fevered stupor, *How does she so deftly do that with me in the bed?*

Her next recollection was an elderly gentleman with a long white beard bending over her. His breath smelled of garlic. He spoke in hushed tones to Gideon as her husband nodded or shook his head in response. The physician never touched her but gave instructions to Hasina to do this or that—uncover her or cover her or sponge her face or dry her off or prod her abdomen. He handed Hasina a pouch with some herbs which he directed the servant to brew and give to Zahava every hour. Then the men left the room.

The vile tasting concoction did lower her fever but did not stop the bleeding. Much as she had tried to hope, she was not surprised. She had not really believed this physician could help her—no one had been able to. It was hopeless, a waste of time and money.

The return trip was a blur. Grateful for the carrying chair, Zahava slept most of the time in a half-reclining position surrounded by pillows. The jostling of the chair fell into a rhythmic pattern that lulled her to sleep. Clip-clip-clip-clop. Clip-clip-clip-clop.

No one stood outside to greet them. At Zahava's insistence, Gideon had not sent a servant ahead to alert Moshe and Yenta of their arrival time. She wanted no inquiries and questions about the physician's findings from the family—especially from Yenta.

Hasina assisted Zahava from her mount. Once on the ground, Zahava leaned on her servant and moved toward the stairs which wound around from the back side of the house to her quarters.

Gideon started after her, but Yenta appeared at that moment and erected a wall between them with her words. "Glad you are back, son." Her narrowed eyes darted toward Zahava leaning on Hasina's arm as they ascended the stairs. "I pray your trip was successful." Without waiting for an answer, she turned to go back inside, calling over her shoulder, "The evening meal awaits. Go dip in the *mikveh*, Gideon, so you can join us." No touching. No contact until he went through the cleansing ritual.

Zahava's vision, blurred from the tears stinging her eyes, blinded her as she stumbled on the top step. The icy stare of rejection from Yenta pierced her heart like thorns. Threatening sobs racked her frail frame as Hasina helped her rise from her knees. As she regained her balance, she caught a glimpse of Gideon rushing to the bottom of the stairs, hesitating with one foot on the first step. The other in the dust of the courtyard. He touched his hand to his chest, but Zahava ignored his gesture and continued to her quarters.

Hasina gently lowered Zahava to her bed and removed her outer clothing. "You still feel feverish to me. Would you like me to sponge you off with some perfumed water and oil?"

Zahava nodded and covered her eyes with her arm, still sniveling. Without taking her arm from her face, she asked, "Is there wine?"

"Yes, Mistress."

"Would you pour me some, please?"

Hasina did not answer, but Zahava heard the clank of the pitcher against the goblet and then the sloshing of the drink as the servant filled the container. "Does my mistress want me to dilute her drink this evening?"

Zahava sat up and took a sip. It was strong. Too strong for her taste ordinarily. But not this evening. "No, it's fine. Thank you." She upended the goblet and took a long, deep drink, hoping the wine would carry her away. She wanted to fall into an intoxicated sleep—a dreamless slumber from which she might never awake. What she had to face every morning had become more than she could bear.

She finished the goblet and reached for another. The room spun around her. She lay back on her pillows and let the black oblivion of sleep claim her.

When she awoke the next morning, it was with a vengeance as the sun cut through the archways in Zahava's room. Her head throbbed, and her body ached. Hasina set a tray of bread, fruit, and cheese on the table and hastened to her side. "Is my mistress ready to eat?"

Zahava moaned and turned her head. "No, take it away. Just give me something to drink."

"You must eat something. You will get sick."

"I *am* sick!" Zahava snapped at Hasina. "And I am never going to get well. I might as well face it." Her chin quivered, and she bit down on her lip to stop the trembling. "I wish I could simply disappear, just go away, so Gideon could get on with his life. I'm of no use to anybody."

The servant calmly went about her morning duties,

ignoring Zahava's outburst. "There are fresh mangos this morning, ripe and sweet."

Zahava stared into the sunlight dancing off the water in the fountain in the courtyard. "I'm ready."

Hasina lifted the tray. "I'm glad to hear that. You need some nourishment."

"No, not that. I mean I'm ready to try some of your Egyptian remedies."

Hasina looked intently at her with her dark eyes—eyes so dark one could not distinguish the pupil from the iris. Black, fringed with thick eyelashes. She set the tray on the table beside Zahava's bed. "Very well. Whatever you wish."

"When can we begin?"

Hasina smiled and dipped her head ever so slightly. "As soon as you eat your breakfast."

chapter 10

Zahava lay on her bed, quivering from the inside out, from her belly to her fingertips down to her toes. Her hair had been braided and twisted on top of her head, which was swathed in a turban. Hasina set a bowl of warm water on the table, along with towels, oils, and a jar of sugar paste. A small sharp obsidian knife lay beside the bowl of water. A thin blanket covered Zahava's nakedness, but still she shivered.

Hasina lay her hand on Zahava's shoulder and spoke softly. "None of this will be painful. It is simply for cleanliness. Be at peace."

But Zahava was not trembling from fear of pain or from the cold. Her trepidation was terror of disobeying the Law. The words of *Torah* romped through her mind. *You must not do as they do in Egypt, where you used to live, and you must not do as they do in the land of Canaan, where I am bringing you. Do not follow their practices.*

She took a deep breath and looked up at Hasina. "Go ahead with your procedure. I am *karat* already—unclean, untouchable, cut off. If I am to be deemed unclean through no fault of my own, I might as well try to find a cure any way I can—disobedient or not." Closing her eyes, she motioned with a weak wave of her hand. "Proceed."

Hasina tilted the flask of olive oil and poured the fragrant ointment into her hands. The spicy scent of cassia and myrrh filled Zahava's nostrils and calmed her nerves. She ceased trembling.

"Lift your arms over your head."

Zahava stretched her arms toward the wall. Hasina applied the oil, beginning with the tips of her fingers, down her arms and armpits, over her breasts, down the torso of her body, her legs and then ended by massaging her feet. Zahava could sense the tension leaving her body.

"Now turn onto your stomach."

Zahava did as instructed. Hasina repeated the process.

The servant set the flask of oil on the table and picked up the jar of sugar paste. She covered Zahava's back, buttocks and legs with the sugar paste, then wiped it down with one of the towels. Taking the knife, she scraped areas which were not yet rid of body hair. Again, the servant poured the oil over her body and rubbed it down. "Turn back over please."

Zahava turned over and lifted her arms above her head ~57 without being told to do so. She chewed on the inside of her cheek as Hasina picked up the knife. The servant held the knife in her hand and bent over her. Zahava flinched.

Hasina raised up and rested the blade of the knife in her hand. "I'll shave first on this side, then use the sugar paste to exfoliate any excess hair."

Zahava nodded and closed her eyes once again. "I'm ready."

Hasina shaved Zahava's underarms, then her belly and private area. Her legs were last. Hasina smeared the remainder of the sugar paste over her entire body, wiped it down, then swathed her body once more with the oil. She covered Zahava with the blanket.

Zahava sighed and leaned up on one elbow, covering herself with the blanket. "Are we finished?"

Hasina smiled. "That's just the cleansing part. Now I need to apply the acacia poultice."

"Oh." Zahava lay back down. She felt clean, slick, and… vulnerable, perhaps? Akin to what she would experience coming out of the *mikveh*, but different.

"Just relax while I heat the poultice."

"No poking or prodding?" Zahava closed her eyes once again. "I don't think I can endure any more of that kind of thing. I'm so weary of—"

"No, not at all. I'll simply lay the poultice on your abdomen until it cools, then I'll apply another. We'll alternate the warm poultices all night to stop the bleeding."

"You'll stay up with me all night?"

"Yes."

Zahava sat up, holding the blanket beneath her chin and shivering once again. "You are a virtuous woman, Hasina. Thank you. Even though…"

"Even though I am a pagan?" Hasina smiled. "While I am Egyptian, I long ago began to believe in Jehovah God." The servant started a fire in the fireplace. She transferred the herbs into a drawstring bag. "I still treasure my Egyptian culture, but as I listened to the reading of the Scripture in the household year after year and heard of the might of your God, my spirit was stirred. One day it occurred I had little by little begun to believe in your God—quite unbeknownst to me. I now know he is the one true God." She set the clay pot of water in the glowing embers of the fireplace. "I'm not sure when or how it happened, but I do believe in Jehovah God with all my heart."

"Hasina. I had no idea. Why did I not know this?"

Hasina looked down, her thick lashes brushing her cheek. "You never asked me."

"I…uh. Hmm. I suppose I simply assumed that you were still…"

"A pagan?"

Zahava drew a deep breath. "I suppose so." She stared

at the servant. She indeed did not wear on her person any of the typical Egyptian amulets, or replicas of their gods. A white veil covered her head today. Long gold earrings were her only adornment.

"Tell me about the earrings you always wear."

Hasina sat by the fire waiting for the water to boil. She fingered the earrings. "My husband gave them to me. They are all I have from him, so I wear them every day. But I wear them also because they are always moving, alive, shimmering. That's how Jehovah God feels to me—moving in me. Springing to life within me." She looked down. "I do not know if I speak blasphemy."

Zahava had no answer. God did not feel alive to her. She wanted to experience a living God within her spirit too. She found herself hoping her servant's thoughts of God were right.

Hasina stood and picked up the cloth bag from the hearth. "This is hot now." Holding the bag by the drawstring, she lowered it into the boiling water for a few moments, then wrapped it in a towel. "Lie down on your back, and try to relax."

Zahava did as instructed and closed her eyes as Hasina placed the poultice on her abdomen. Zahava drew in a long breath.

"Is it too hot, my lady?"

"No, it's fine." Zahava put her hand over the poultice. "Actually, it feels rather good."

The night passed with Hasina removing the poultices and replacing them with hot ones. Zahava slept off and on, with the shimmering earrings dancing through her dreams. When Zahava awoke in the morning, the servant was gone, and she was alone. She placed her hand on her abdomen. It was tender and pink but not injured in any way. The poultice was gone. Glancing toward the fireplace she saw all the incriminating material had been taken away. Everything looked normal. She stretched with a groan and ran her fingers along her armpit. It was smooth from having been shaven. She was afraid to sit up—afraid of what she anticipated she would encounter on the bed clothing. She rolled onto her side and paused. Heaving a deep sigh, she swung her legs over the edge of the bed and stood, gathering the bed cover around her. She glanced at the linens on the bed.

They were clean. No blood that she could see. Snatching at the sheets and pillows, she searched every inch of them. No blood.

"Hasina! Hasina!" She ran to the archway, clutching the cover around her.

The servant hurried up the stairs, her eyes wide. "What is it, Mistress? Is anything wrong?"

"Wrong? No! Not wrong, but very right. Come and see." Zahava pointed to her bed. "No blood this morning. It's gone. You've worked a miracle. It's gone!"

Hasina raised her hand. "I would caution my mistress not to become excited too hastily. This treatment must continue for seven days." She went to the bed and examined it. A smile creased her face. "But this does appear promising."

"Could it have been this simple? How have all the physicians missed something this simple?"

"Again, I would caution you not to consider yourself cured—just yet. Let us continue the treatment and see what happens. May I be so bold as to say I believe it would be wise not to share this with anyone else, lest it be another dead end?" Hasina looked down. "Forgive me if I have spoken out of turn."

Zahava took Hasina's hands in her own. "Oh, my dear woman. If this indeed works, how could I ever thank you? I would owe you my life."

Hasina pulled away, shaking her head. "I am but your servant. Anything I can do to serve my lady, I am happy to oblige."

Night after night Hasina prepared the poultices and applied them to Zahava's abdomen. Zahava's interrupted sleep was filled with the Egyptian servant floating in and out of her dreams and her reality. The bleeding ceased during the week of treatment and a day or so afterward, but then returned like some kind of retribution, before Zahava could even go to the *mikveh* for cleansing. Gripping the soiled bedclothes in her fists, she fell to her knees and wept bitter tears of despair—desperate, debilitating despair.

chapter 11

"God is mocking me." Zahava gritted her teeth and shook her fist toward the sky. "Why are you doing this to me? For what am I being punished? All I want is to be a wife and mother to my family. Is that so evil?"

The laughter of children beckoned to her from the courtyard. She leaned over the stone wall which encased the balcony of her quarters and watched the cousins, Gideon's nieces and nephews and some of her younger brothers and sisters, as they chased after a new litter of puppies. The black and white bundles of fur scattered as the children ran after them, attempting to capture one. One of the youngest, Luke finally caught a puppy by the hind leg and hauled it into his chubby hands. His little boy giggles of laughter wrenched her heart. He was oblivious he was being watched.

I am not really a part of my family's life. I have been cut out of it until none of the children even know who I am—even though they are the only ones who would not be made unclean by touching me, they are kept from me. I am of no use to my husband or the household. Why am I alive? She looked up to the rooftop. *I could end it all now by simply throwing myself down to the courtyard.*

She gripped the rough edge of the wall. *That would solve the problem. Tonight I will go up to the roof and…I can make it look like an accident. I could be walking, stumble and fall.*

Nobody would guess it was intentional. All of this suffering would be over—all of the vain searching for a cure, and the expense. Then Gideon would be free to remarry.

"Zahava." Gideon's deep voice startled her.

She whirled around from her self-talk to face her beloved. *Did he know what she was contemplating?* "You frightened me." Her heart thumped—not only from being startled. His nearness still caused her heart to quicken. He walked toward her.

Out of habit, she backed away. "What are you doing here?"

"Since when am I not allowed to visit my wife?" His dark eyes bore into hers, anguish reflected in their liquid pools. "You have hidden yourself away the last several days. I have not even caught a glimpse of you. Are you ill?"

An embittered chuckle forced its way out of her throat. "Am I ill? What a question to ask one who is chronically ill. So ill I cannot be with my husband."

"I meant in addition to your…your problem."

"My problem? My problem is quite enough, thank you." She turned her back on him and gritted her teeth.

"Zahava, I'm sorry. There's no need to be angry with me. I miss you. I simply wanted to check and see if you were…" Gideon looked around the room. "Something is different." He turned his head and sniffed. "What's that I smell?"

Zahava faced her husband. "Does it smell bad?"

"No, just different. Like herbs or something."

"Oh, Hasina has been massaging my body with a sugar paste."

"No, it's something else. Herbal. Not perfumed."

"Well, she's been using…using acacia leaves as well. That's all." She flicked her wrist in dismissal.

"No pagan rituals or incantations?"

"No, nothing like that at all. Do you really think I would

63

permit that?"

"I wouldn't, ordinarily, but when one gets desperate, one can sometimes do or think irrationally."

Zahava looked out toward the courtyard. Did Gideon suspect? "Did you know Hasina believes in Jehovah God?"

"She told you that?"

"Yes. She said through the years she has come to believe in the one true God."

"No, I was not aware of it. She takes good care of you, for which I am grateful." Gideon moved closer to her. "We need to talk about something." He leaned with his elbows atop the wall and smiled at the children playing with the puppies.

Gideon pointed at Luke chasing after the scampering puppy which had escaped his grip. "Look at that little one. He thinks he is as big as they are." The children dashed in and out among the trees, squealing and laughing. Luke knelt down, coaxing the animal with a piece of food. "See how clever he is? He knows he mustn't keep chasing the dogs. They will simply run away."

They watched as the puppy waddled toward him and gobbled the morsel Luke held out to him. The boy gathered the puppy in his arms and nestled him in his tunic.

Gideon slapped the ledge of the wall. "Now that's smart, isn't it?"

Zahava smiled. "Yes, dear. Our nephew is brilliant."

"No, really. That is smart for a three-year-old. To reason out that if he kept chasing the puppies, he'd never snag one. He set a trap to capture one. All of the others are still chasing them."

Zahava peered down at the children once again. They were now playing in the dirt, digging with little wooden shovels. "Well, actually I think they've given up." The puppies had gone back to their mother and were languishing in the shade of the stone walkway.

"My point exactly. Luke reasoned out if he kept doing the same thing with no results, that was not productive. So he made another plan." Gideon smiled at his wife. "I'm sure he didn't reason it out like an adult, but he knew he needed to do something different. That's smart."

"Isn't that what we're doing?"

"What?"

"Doing the same thing over and over and expecting different results?"

"What are you talking about?"

"We keep running from physician to physician searching for healing, never finding it, but we keep doing the same thing over and over expecting different results. Is that smart?"

"I suppose not, but I don't know what else to do." Gideon sighed. "Let's sit down. I need to talk to you about something." The two sat on benches on the balcony opposite each other. Zahava straightened a potted palm at the end of the bench. The pot scraped on the floor, slicing through the awkward silence. _65

"My parents are becoming more insistent. They are putting pressure on me to divorce you. I want you to know that I continue to refuse to do so. I will never…"

Zahava listened, anticipating the words, not wanting to hear them, but powerless to stop them. She watched her husband's mouth moving. Words came from his lips sounding like a foreign language, words she thought she would never hear from the love of her life.

"…put you away, divorce you, leave you."

She wanted to cover her ears and run from the room, screaming. But she sat, rooted to the bench, unable to move, and stared at him as one struck mute.

He paused, searching her face for a response, his eyes

reddened with tears. He leaned forward, his elbows on his knees, his hands clasped in front of him. "This is not what I intend to do, but I wanted you to know I am getting increased pressure to go to the priest for a divorce. If you hear talk in the house, just ignore it." He hung his head and swiped at his eyes.

She longed to reach out to him and comfort him. He was in as much torment as she. The state of her health had become the ultimate truth of her life, the determining force of her destiny. Her past and future blended into a present from which she could not escape. She stood, suddenly feeling very old, and walked away from Gideon. "Do what you need to do. I understand. Please leave now."

Gideon jumped from the bench and caught hold of her arm. "Don't walk away from me."

Zahava stared at his hand on her arm—his strong hand, the back of it broad and tanned. That very act made him unclean, unable to go to Temple until he cleansed himself in the *mikveh*. That innocent act of touching his own wife. She longed to clutch his hand in her own and smother it with kisses. She longed to fall into his arms and feel the warmth of his breath on her cheek as it grew rapid and heavy. She longed to lie beside him and feel his caress.

But what she did was throw his arm off of her own and run from him. She would not make the mistake again of being weak and causing him to be *karat*. The priest might not be as lenient if it happened again. She ran to the darkened interior of her room.

"Zahava, wait."

She paused but remained with her back to her husband. "Please leave. I understand your dilemma. Do what you need to do."

Gideon followed her and, putting his hands on her shoulders, turned her around to face him. "I've already touched you. Let me hold you—just hold you."

Zahava pushed away. "No, Gideon. It's too wrenching to want you and be unable to have you. It makes it worse for me." She stepped back. "I want you to go. It's already been five years wasted. I want you to do what you must do to get on with your life. If you truly love me, you must do this."

Gideon shook his head, his eyes drooping from sadness. "I will never leave you." He hesitated, took a few steps toward the stairs, then turned back. "There's one more thing."

Zahava waited, overcome with emotion, unable to speak.

"My parents have offered to build you a small house in the country, so you can have your privacy."

Zahava felt as if he had thrown cold water in her face. She could not catch her breath. "My…my privacy?" She sat down at her vanity, her heart seeming to jump from her chest. "What you are saying is I am being put away from the family, out of sight, so I can no longer be an embarrassment to you." She gripped her hands together in her lap to keep them from trembling. "And you agreed to this?"

"I have no choice. It's either this or you will continue to be spurned by my family. When my father first offered the proposal, I was adamantly against it and refused to even consider it. But when I thought about it, I realized this gives us a way to be together, in a manner of speaking, without prying eyes and ears. You may take Hasina with you. I will make sure it is a house that will meet every need you might have." He smiled and popped his knuckles. "I will build you a beautiful house of your own."

He knelt in front of her and took her hands in his own. Capturing her with his eyes, he touched her chin. "I love you, Zahava, and I will never stop loving you. God will make a way for us."

"Please leave, Gideon. I have much to think about." Her

voice was a hoarse whisper. "And I'm very tired."

Gideon rose and touched his chest. Zahava returned his lover's gesture but remained seated as he went down the stairs. She heard his footsteps hesitate at one point on the steps. She held her breath, praying he would not come back. After a moment they resumed, and he went on down.

Hasina came into the room, but Zahava waved her off. "Go on about your chores. I think I'll go to bed. I'm just so weary." She lay down on her bed and fell to sleep quickly.

She awoke sometime during the night. She sat up and listened. The house was silent except for Hasina's heavy breathing as she lay on her pallet beside Zahava's bed. Zahava swung her legs over the side of the bed, opposite where Hasina slept, and stood. She gathered her cloak around her and tiptoed out of the room toward the stairs going to the roof.

Hasina turned over and coughed. Zahava froze until Hasina lay quiet again. Then she made her way to the rooftop and looked down at the dark and silent courtyard. Not a sound. No one awake except her.

No one would know until morning.

chapter 12

Zahava stood on her toes and peered over the wall surrounding the roof. Strange. She'd never noticed before how high the wall was. She would have to stand on something to climb over it. Several benches sat scattered about, but they were made from heavy stone. She'd never be able to move them. Then she spied one of the chairs Gideon had purchased from the carpenter in Nazareth. He must have decided to keep one for himself. It sat beside a large potted palm in the corner. She lifted it and started toward the wall. The chair was heavier than she remembered. She set it down and pulled it the rest of the way, wincing as the legs scraped across the floor.

She stopped. Listened. The stillness of the night pressed upon her, suffocating her, ringing in her ears. A dog barked in the distance. The mother of the puppies returned the bark—once, twice—then fell silent. She held her breath as the night grew still once more. Her breath came in quick, small gasps. Her heart thudded.

She sat in the chair, weak-kneed and shivering, in spite of the warm night.

What was she doing? Why was she even thinking the unthinkable? Because she was of no use to anybody—herself or her husband. She was a burden, a liability. Gideon would never put her away legally. He loved her too much. She knew that. But in essence they were planning to put her away, only they were covering the deed up with a lovely country estate. Away so no one would be contaminated by her. Away so she could no longer be a disgrace to the family. Away so perhaps Moshe and Yenta could persuade Gideon to divorce her as his contact with her would be less and less.

Well, she would put herself away for them before they went to all that expense.

The chair seemed to fit her body perfectly. It was comfortable and soothing. She rose and scooted it closer to the wall. Holding on to the back of the chair with one hand, she raised her skirt and stepped onto the seat. Could she lift herself up high enough to sit on the ledge then push herself over? The legs of the chair teetered unevenly on the floor. She tried to lift herself to the ledge but didn't have enough strength in her arms to get all the way up. Trying again, she kicked her legs, caught the top of the chair with her toe and toppled it over.

It clattered to the floor.

Hanging over the ledge on her stomach, she tried to swing her leg up to the top of the wall but failed and had to let go. She fell to the floor on top of the chair, knocking the breath out of her.

"Mistress?" Hasina, with a lighted oil lamp in her hand, ran to Zahava and stooped over her. "Are you injured? What are you doing up here?" She looked at the toppled chair and frowned.

Zahava sat with her back against the wall. "I…I…just… couldn't sleep and came up for some fresh air." Her voice sounded weak and unconvincing.

Hasina set the lamp down on a nearby table and assisted Zahava as she struggled to her feet. She righted the chair and brought it close to the table. "Please, Mistress. Sit down for a moment. You are trembling."

Zahava sat in the chair and dropped her head in her hands. "Oh, Hasina. Gideon told me this evening that his family wants him to put me away."

"A divorce?"

"No, not legally, but they want to move me out. Build a separate house and keep m—me isolated from the family." She wiped her tears away with the back of her hand.

"If it please my mistress, may I speak?"

Zahava nodded, sniveling.

"This may be better until a cure is found. The master can come to see you without pressure. You would feel freer." Hasina looked down. "I am assuming I would go with you."

"Yes, of course."

"At least your husband does not want to divorce you." Hasina opened the doors of a small cabinet against the wall and removed a towel. She handed it to Zahava and stepped back with her hands folded in front of her. "It is my observation that your husband loves you very much. He is simply caught between his parents and his wife."

Zahava wiped her nose. She looked up at Hasina and blurted out between sobs, "I know that. The only an—answer is for me to be healed or…"

Hasina looked toward the wall. She hesitated for an eternity of moments before speaking. Her soft, thickly accented voice carried no condemnation, only wisdom. "What you have been contemplating is no solution. Think of the heartache and shame such an act would bring to Gideon and your family." The tall, slender woman walked to the wall with the grace of a gazelle and looked over. "He would never get over it."

Zahava put her head in her hands and wept, moans emanating from her body as though squeezed out by an unseen force. "I have no hope. I don't know what else to do. I pray and pray, but God does not answer. I am useless to my husband. Why doesn't God answer?"

"I believe God is at work even when we cannot see the results. We have to trust him."

Zahava took a deep breath and patted her cheeks with the cloth. "Now I am learning from you about Jehovah God, instead of you learning from me."

"Please forgive me. I mean no disrespect."

Zahava rose. "I did not receive it as disrespect. Quite the opposite."

Both women turned as a rustle on the stairs interrupted their conversation. Gideon topped the stairs in his tunic, barefooted, his abundant dark curls in complete disarray. "I heard something. Is anything amiss?" His glance darted around the roof.

Zahava reached out for the servant's arm. "No, dear, nothing is amiss. I couldn't sleep, so we came up for some fresh air."

"I heard a noise and grabbed this on the way up." He held a large stick in his hand, chuckling. "Not that it would have been that effective. However, everything seems to be in place." He glanced from corner to corner of the rooftop.

Hasina spoke. "It was my fault. I was moving the chair over to the table for my mistress to rest, and I carelessly knocked it over. I apologize."

"That must have been what I heard." He looked at Zahava. "You are certain you are well?"

"As well as can be expected. Come, Hasina. I think I can sleep now." The two women moved toward Gideon and the stairs. They stopped in front of him. Zahava wanted to run her fingers through his thick hair, kiss him, and snuggle into his strong arms. But she could not. "I will agree to the country house. Do what you must. Good night, Gideon." She touched her hand to her heart and descended the stairs with Hasina, leaving Gideon behind on the rooftop, shifting his would-be weapon from one hand to the other.

The country house proved to be a viable solution, and Zahava settled into its comforts with Hasina. At first, Gideon came nearly every day, more than he had visited her quarters in the main house. But the demands of the family business and the travel back and forth became burdensome to deal with.

Days between visits turned into weeks.

And without his regular company, time ceased to have meaning. Weeks melted into months, and months trudged their way into years. Zahava watched them slide by from her window, her limbs growing ever weaker. Year by agonizing year.

She watched him dismount from his donkey now, watched him walk toward the door. He still looked young in his mid-thirties, while she felt ancient. Twelve years of bleeding had taken her strength and her youth. She listened for his voice as he greeted Hasina.

He did keep his word that he would not divorce Zahava, she would grant him that. And he continued to search for a cure. Sometimes she would comply with his wishes to see this physician or that one, but no one could offer a permanent cure. Hasina continued the acacia poultices for a time. They offered some relief for a few days, but the bleeding would always return.

But when she heard him mention another healer today, she gathered the strength to stomp from the room. "No more!"

Gideon blinked his eyes at her outburst and backed up

toward the door.

Zahava clutched her robe tight, seeking its warmth. "I'm sick of hearing 'Arise from thy flux,' after each procedure. Over and over again I complied with their bizarre instructions. And I would arise, but still the flux followed me. All the ridiculous things I've had to do including drinking concoctions made from stags' horns and the livers of frogs and who knows what else has come to an end. No more." She paced in front of her husband. "I'm done. All I do is get weaker. I never get stronger and better. I shall never go to another physician—never again! Do you hear me? Never again!" She was clenching her fists and shouting by this point.

"But this is different, Zahava. This man is not a physician, but a healer, a miracle worker—this man is truly healing people simply with a touch." He popped his knuckles. "Some say he is the Messiah."

"Gideon, you're talking out of your head now—snatching at straws." Her energy depleted, she sat on the chair she had brought with her from the balcony at the main house. A blanket lay across the rungs on the back of the chair which she now drew across her shoulders. She stayed chilled most of the time these days. "I'll not go to anyone else. Just leave me be." She turned sideways in the chair and put her elbow on the back of it, resting her chin in her hand. As she watched him move, love still made her heart thump. She could never stay angry with him. "You say he is a healer?"

Gideon sat down across from her. "He healed a paralytic right here in Capernaum a few weeks ago."

"He did? Were you present? Did you witness it?"

"No, but I've talked to people who did."

She wound a thread from the blanket around her finger. "Hmm. What happened?"

"He was teaching at Peter's house. You know Peter, the fisherman."

Zahava nodded, avoiding his eyes, concentrating on the thread around her finger. "I know who he is."

"Evidently he has identified himself with this man and is one of his followers. Be that as it may, the man was teaching at Peter's house and there was quite a crowd, I hear. Some men brought a friend to the house who was paralyzed, carried him on his pallet. The man couldn't even get there on his own. But when they arrived, there was such a crowd they couldn't get through to him. So…" Gideon paused and chuckled. "These were some determined friends. They went up the outside stairs to the roof, lugging their paralyzed friend up on his bed and busted a hole in the roof so they could lower the friend down in front of… " He stopped and looked at Zahava.

"What? Tell me what happened."

"Well, the man was healed. Picked up his own bed and walked away from the scene. But there's something else you need to know about this."

"What is it?" Zahava unwound the thread and looked at Gideon.

"I've heard him teach since then. After I heard about this miraculous healing, I heard he was teaching one day down by the seashore, and I went to hear him for myself. He speaks like no other rabbi I've ever heard. He speaks with authority and compassion. I believe he is genuine."

"That's what I need to know? That the man is genuine?"
"No—well, yes. I mean, you need to know he speaks truth, but what I wanted to tell you is the man who is stirring up the countryside with his teaching and his healing is the carpenter from Nazareth." Gideon stood, popping his knuckles, then squared his shoulders. "Zahava, the man is Jesus."

chapter 13

Zahava stared at Gideon. "That nice young man who made the chairs for us?" She stood abruptly, pulling the blanket with her, and turned around to stare at the chair. The chair in which she always seemed to sit when she trying to get comfortable. "The carpenter from Nazareth? He is healing people?" The young man who told her that God always answers prayer in his own time?

Gideon nodded. "That's what I hear."

"I don't believe it. He was a nice young man, but a healer? The Messiah?"

"Let me take you to him. What could it hurt? The worst thing that could happen would be once again you wouldn't be healed. Can you not take one more chance?"

"I cannot go through this again, Gideon." Tears stung the back of her eyelids. "To have my hopes dashed over and over is just too much."

Her still handsome husband stepped toward her. Zahava moved behind the chair away from him using it has a barrier between them. Gideon, having none of it, flung the chair aside and gathered her in his arms. "I am taking you to him."

Zahava shrunk away from his display of force and dissolved in a barrage of tears. "Nooo, Gideon." Her whole body shook, and her knees buckled. "Don't. I can't." She feebly pushed against him, then fell limp in his arms.

Gideon held her up and pressed his cheek to hers. He

whispered in her ear. "Yes, you can. You can make this one last effort. If this doesn't work, I won't insist on any more physicians, but I'm taking you to see Jesus." He turned to Hasina. "Get her clothes, and help me clean her up. I'm taking her to him."

Zahava stared at Gideon as she allowed Hasina to take her to the other room. His eyes were different—a steady light of hope glimmered from them. Something strong, more determined. He took a basin from the table and tossed the liquid outside. Lifting the water pot from beside the door, he poured fresh water into the basin and brought it to Hasina. The servant pulled a fresh robe from a peg on the wall and laid it on the bed. She removed Zahava's headpiece and brushed Zahava's thinning hair, braiding it quickly into a knot.

Zahava clutched Hasina's arm. "Do I look fit for my husband? I feel withered, wrinkled, used up."

"My mistress will be fine. Here." She handed Zahava the gold bracelet Gideon had given her years before.

Zahava's wrist had grown so small she could hardly keep it from slipping off. "The earrings too. I want to wear the earrings." Hasina opened a carved box which held Zahava's jewelry, most of it seldom worn anymore. She found the large jade-studded earrings and handed them to Zahava, but Zahava's hands trembled so she couldn't thread the thin gold wire through her ear.

"Here, Mistress. Let me do it for you." Hasina gently inserted the earrings.

Gideon's wide smile greeted her as they emerged from the house. He touched his chest and held out his hand for her. Faithful Gideon. Zahava felt a rise of hope in her own spirit, born of what she sensed in her husband—a new faith, a new belief.

Gideon lifted Zahava onto a donkey into the carrying

chair that Jesus had made for her years before. He mounted his donkey and rode beside her, holding the reins, leading her animal. Hasina walked alongside her, with her hand on the edge of the carrying chair, steadying it. Zahava hung on to the arms of the chair, fearful in her weakened condition she would not even be able to endure the short trip to the outskirts of the village.

Gideon stopped the donkeys. "I don't know where to find Jesus, but let's start by going to Peter's house. I know where he lives. Perhaps that's where he is staying."

Zahava nodded. Her headdress had fallen around her shoulders, and she pulled it over her head. "I must look a mess."

Gideon dismounted and walked to her donkey. He smiled at her. "You are still beautiful to me."

"You would have to be blind to say that. My skin is sallow; I'm losing my hair; I'm skin and bones. I'm not only sick, I've grown old." Zahava pulled her cloak around her.

"But I see the young, vibrant, beautiful wife that I married so many years ago. You are still there. I see it in your eyes." Gideon took hold of her donkey's bridle. "And we will get that Zahava back."

They turned down a narrow side street and walked between rows of vendors hawking their wares—rugs, jewelry, as well as colorful fruits and vegetables in bins and carts. The marketplace teemed with people of all ages, children chasing one another in tag, dogs barking. Gideon pointed toward the end of the street. "Peter's house is just around the bend in the road." As they turned the corner, a large house sat at the end of the street.

Gideon tied their donkeys to a hitching post in front and went to the door. A woman answered. Zahava saw her shake her head and point back toward the marketplace. Gideon returned to them. Smiling, he pointed to a pile of rubble beside the front of the house. "That must be the mess left from the hole in the roof." He chuckled and unhitched the donkeys.

Anxiety—or perhaps anticipation—gripped her. "Well? Where is he? Where is Jesus?"

"That was Peter's wife who answered the door. She said Jesus and his disciples have gone to the village."

Zahava's heart plunged. "We've missed him?" They had missed their opportunity.

"She said they've not been gone long. Perhaps we can catch up with him." Gideon mounted his donkey and grabbed the bridle of Zahava's. "Come on. We will find him." He spurred the small animal to a trot as they hurried back toward the marketplace.

Hasina held on to her headpiece and ran beside them, her sandaled feet stirring up the dust along with the donkeys. Soon Gideon and Zahava lost Hasina in the crowd. "Wait, Gideon! Hasina is not with us."

"We cannot wait for her. We'll find her later. We've got to catch up with Jesus." Gideon wound his way through the streets, stretching his neck, looking for the man and his party. Finally near the opposite end of town, Gideon spotted a throng of people moving along slowly. "I see a crowd ahead. That must be them."

They slowed their donkeys to a walk, then Gideon dismounted and assisted Zahava off her donkey.

They bumped up against a tall man with a bushy beard and asked him what was drawing the crowd. The man looked at Gideon and Zahava and pointed to the center. "It's that man, Jesus, who is healing all sorts of illnesses. People are always clamoring to get to him. He can hardly walk from place to place without being smothered by people needing to be healed." He scoffed. "The rest are simply curious onlookers—like me." The man turned and walked away. "I need to get back to work."

Gideon shielded Zahava in his arms and attempted to make a way through the crowd, but there were too many people. The pushing and shoving kept them at the edge of the mob. Exasperated, he propelled her in a different direction. "Let's go to the other side."

A shout rose from the commotion as a man pushed his way past them. His face, contorted by panic, barreled his way through the crowd. "My daughter. Jesus, my daughter is dying. You must come with me now!" The clamor intensified as the man fell on his knees in front of Jesus and compelled the man to go with him.

"That's Jairus." Gideon had mentioned him before. He was the director of the synagogue, a man with much influence in the village. They watched the demeanor of the group change even as their direction changed. "We've missed our chance."

"No, wait, Gideon. I know how I can get to him." She pushed away from him. "Let go of me."

"What do you intend to do? You are too weak to fight this crowd by yourself."

"I won't have to, but I must go to the healer by myself." She pulled the edge of her headdress from her shoulder. "I am unclean. They will part and make a way for me."

Gideon's eyes widened as he slowly shook his head. "I won't allow you to be subjected to that humiliation." He put his arm around her shoulders and drew her back to him. "I will go with you."

"No, I must expose my shame in order to be healed. I can get to him, but I have to do it by myself." She looked into his eyes. "I saw his face. I remember that face. I know he can heal me. Wait here for me."

"But…"

"Wait for me." Zahava turned her back on her husband.

Holding the edge of her headpiece over her face with one hand, leaving only her eyes showing, and holding the other hand in front of her, she called out, "Unclean! Unclean!"

Startled faces turned her way as she walked toward the crowd. One by one they stepped aside to let her pass by, gathering their children to their sides and pulling their robes around their shoulders.

chapter 14

The crowd swallowed Zahava as she made her way toward the center of the commotion. Her knees weakened and quivered, and she stumbled, falling into the dust. No one reached to help her up. No one offered an outstretched hand. A bubble of silence surrounded her, although she could hear the din of the throng ahead. She managed to get to her feet and continued to cry out, "Unclean! Unclean!"

Whispers assaulted her ears. Whispers of, "Move away. Don't touch her. She's unclean. Get back!"

Then a kind voice. "Make a way for her to get through. She needs to get to Jesus." A kindly, older gentleman with a close-cut gray beard nodded at her and smiled. "Make your way to him, child. Keep moving. He's just ahead."

The crowd closed in around her again, and she lost sight of Jesus. Then just ahead she thought she could see the top of his head. A cluster of men surrounded him, ushering him along the narrow street. Her foot became entangled in her robe, tossing her to the ground again. This time it knocked the breath out of her. She couldn't get up. The press of the crowd was too much, above her, surrounding her. Feet shuffled all around her—sandaled dusty feet, men and women, children. A dog scampered in and out through the legs of the people. Everyone seemed to be leaning forward.

Broken sentences reached her. "There—"

"That's him."

"Where?"

"I can't see him."

She continued her zig-zagging on her hands and knees, through the groping mass of people. Rocks and gravel scraped her hands. By the time she got to the front of the crowd where she could see the man, he was almost past her. But she could see the side of his face as he turned to first one and then another in the crowd. People reached out and touched his hand, his arm, and he, in turn, greeted them one by one. Said a word to each one grasping for him.

It was him, the young man they had met in Nazareth all those years ago. He had matured, but it was the same man. The one who had made with such care the chairs that held her. The man who had promised Jehovah God would not fail.

Was this the day she had been longing for all these years? ~83 Would this be the day of her healing? Was he truly a healer? Fear descended on her, palpable, black and evil, gripping her mind with icy fingers. *Who do you think you are? You are unclean, unworthy, only a woman.*

For a split second, she withdrew.

But if she could just get to him. If…if she could just *touch* him. She crawled closer. She was propelled forward. Now she was behind him.

She must get to him!

He was talking to everyone who approached him. If she could just reach out to him. That was all it would take, she knew it in her soul. One touch, one forbidden touch, and he could heal her.

She stretched as far as she could, almost reaching him. Just a bit farther…

Her hand fell short, and her fingers clutched only at the tassel on the corner of his robe. The crowd closed in around her, swallowing Jesus up as he moved forward. Her bracelet came off her wrist, and as she scratched in the dirt to retrieve it, something that felt like warm honey surged through her body—beginning with her fingers which touched the robe of Jesus, flowing to every limb and joint. The sensation dazed her. She blinked her eyes, not able to see for a moment. Fumbling for her headdress, she gasped for breath.

"Who touched me?" The deep, mellow voice of Jesus cut through the rabble. The undulating motion of the mass seemed to stop, and a hush settled on the crowd. No one stepped forward.

The man Zahava recognized as Peter spoke up. "Master, there are dozens of people surrounding you. They are touching you on every side. What do you mean, 'Who touched me?'"

"Someone did touch me. I felt the healing power go out of me." He perused the faces of the people circled about him. "Who touched me?"

She was found out. She would have to expose herself. A feeling of guilt for breaking the Law in that instant she touched him flashed through her mind, but she ignored it. She pushed herself to her feet and took a step toward him. Strength flooded through her like waves of the sea coming to shore. The waves washed over her, cleansing and filling her. She inhaled a deep breath of fresh air.

Healed! She knew it immediately. She fell at Jesus's feet, trembling, consumed with awe. "It was I, Master. I touched the tassel on your robe. I've been sick for twelve years and thought if I could just...get...to you, that you would heal me." She lowered her head. "Physician after physician tried to cure me—to no avail. Every treatment, every concoction, every potion failed. My husband spent all of our money seeking a cure. We prayed and prayed, but

God never answered."

She looked back up at him. He extended his hand to her and helped her rise to her feet. She clasped his hand in both of hers and covered it with kisses. He touched her cheek. "Don't you remember? That day in Nazareth, I told you God always answers our prayers, Zahava."

And she did remember. Of course she remembered—but how was it he did?

She stared at him. "I sensed healing pour over my body the moment I touched your robe." She continued to clutch his hands. "I am healed. Thank you, thank you, thank you." Tears flowed down her cheeks, making a dirty path through the dust on her face.

Jesus wiped the tears away with the tip of his finger. "Daughter, you took a risk trusting me, and now you are healed and whole. Go, and be at peace."

She didn't want him to leave her, but he withdrew and went on his way. The crowd left her behind as they moved down the road. ~85

"Zahava!" Gideon, with Hasina trailing behind him, elbowed his way through the crowd and hurried to her side. He encircled her in his arms. "I saw it all. He did heal you. He did, didn't he?" Gideon held her at arm's length and looked at her. He traced his finger along her jawline. "Your...your skin. It is glowing. Your youth has returned." He hugged her, squeezing the breath from her, laughing and twirling her around like a child. "I knew it. I knew if we could just get you to him, you would be healed."

They threw back their heads and laughed together like they used to do when they were young.

Hasina watched the couple in their merriment, a smile creasing her face. Zahava grabbed the servant's hands. "It's over, Hasina. We finally found a cure. It's over. No more poultices."

"Yes, Mistress. It's finally over. God answered our prayers."

The trio returned to where the donkeys were tied—Gideon and Zahava, arm in arm. Loyal Hasina at their side. Zahava stopped, took both of Gideon's hands and pressed her cheek to them. "Gideon, I am overwhelmed with my love for you. You never gave up. You didn't put me away or divorce me. I shall be forever grateful." Emotion tightened her throat, and she choked back a sob.

"How could I have done that? You are the love of my life. I knew we would find a cure one day. How could I abandon you?" With his hand still entwined in hers, he touched his heart. "You have always had my heart." He leaned down and kissed her gently.

Zahava felt as giddy as she had on their wedding day, but it was different. Mature, wiser, grounded.

Like a lightning bolt, a thought zig-zagged a path through her mind. The dream! She grabbed hold of Gideon's arms and shook him. "Gideon, the dream. The dream!"

He took her hands from his arms and held them. "What about the dream?"

"Now I understand it. The dream was telling me all along what I needed to do. All those nights, struggling through the blood in the dream—and through a crowd of people, a crowd of people, Gideon." She motioned to the crowd still visible as they followed Jesus. "Fighting my way through a mass of people to reach someone or something in the distance who could help me. It was him, the Messiah, I was trying to reach. I knew someone could help me. I just couldn't get to him. Didn't know who he was, but I knew somebody could help me." She shook her head. "Why did I know that intuitively in my heart?"

Hasina, with unusual boldness in her voice, spoke up. "Our God put it in your heart."

Zahava smiled at her servant, her companion, her friend. "I believe you are right, dear one. I do believe you are right." She looked at Gideon. "What shall we do now?"

"I suppose we'll need to go to the priest to have you declared clean and healed, and go to the *mikveh*, both of us. But after that, it's very simple. We go home and fill that little country house with lots of babies. Our babies. Yours and mine."

Zahava patted Gideon's hand which she held in her own. "We're getting a rather late start on raising a family."

Gideon shook his head and smiled. "Don't be concerned about that. God's timing is perfect. Remember Abraham and Sarah."

This time Zahava smiled at the reminder.

Discussion Questions

1.   A chronic disease is not only difficult for the victim, but for the family as well. If you are in a group discussion, talk about the reactions and responses of the different members of Zahava's family to her illness. If you are doing an individual study, write out your answers.
- Gideon
- Hasina
- Lois
- Yenta

2.   Has there ever been a member of your family who had a life-threatening or long-term illness? How did you react?

3.   Do you think Zahava's cynicism toward God was justified, understandable? Why or why not?

4.   Zahava met Jesus years before she reached out to him for healing. Jesus even took care of a need before she came to him as the Messiah. Compare and contrast your experience of coming to know God with hers. Was God taking care of your needs before you came to know Jesus as your Savior?

5.   Let's play "just pretend" and ask some "what if" questions. (You know, fiction writers do that all the time.☺) What if Zahava had missed touching the robe by just inches. Do you think she would still have

been healed?

What if she hadn't been healed physically? Do you think she would have been healed spiritually?

6.   When we were in our mid-thirties, my husband was diagnosed with a long-term, incurable disease. But God healed him through the laying on of hands, anointing of oil and prayer of a brother in the Lord. My husband was asleep in the hospital—didn't even know our friend had come in and prayed over him. We have the medical records that he had this disease, and now no longer has it, complete with xrays. Has there ever been a bona-fide, medically recorded miracle of healing in your family? What was it and how did God orchestrate the healing?

7.   Has there ever been a case in your family when God chose not to heal? How did you respond to that situation?

In the final analysis, God is good no matter what path he chooses for us. Close in prayer thanking him for his goodness and whatever circumstances you find yourself in.

Don't miss the other titles in the Hidden Faces Series

Trapped: The Adulterous Woman
Available now!

Alone: The Woman at the Well
Available now!

Broken: The Woman who Anointed Jesus's Feet
Available now!

And the compilation
of all 4 novellas
Hidden Faces: Portraits of Namelss Women in the Gospels